a **NICK**® cookbook

# STIR
# SQUIRT
# SIZZLE

chronicle books · san francisco

Nickelodeon, Rugrats, Nickelodeon Rocket Power, The Wild Thornberrys, SpongeBob SquarePants,
Hey Arnold, The Adventures of Jimmy Neutron: Boy Genius, Fairly OddParents, and all related titles,
logos, and characters are trademarks of Viacom International, Inc. Rugrats, Nickelodeon Rocket
Power, and The Wild Thornberrys created by Klasky Csupo, Inc.
SpongeBob SquarePants created by Stephen Hillenburg.
Hey Arnold created by Craig Bartlett. Fairly OddParents created by Butch Hartman.

Green Slime Birthday Cake recipe reprinted with permission from *Nickelodeon Magazine*.

Photos on pages 14, 15, 32, 33, 36, 38, 39, 40, 41, 44, 45, 46, 47, 50, 51, and 56
by Sheri Giblin. Food styling by EK Food Productions: Erin Quon and Kim Kocecny,
Prop styling by Leigh Noe. Photo Assistant, Selena Aument.

Book design by Sara Gillingham.
Manufactured in China.

Library of Congress Cataloging-in-Publication Data
Stir, squirt, sizzle : a Nick cookbook.
p. cm.
Summary: Characters from "Rugrats," "The Wild Thornberrys," "SpongeBob SquarePants," and other
Nickelodeon television shows present their favorite recipes, including Bikini Bottom Butterscotch
Brownies, Reggie Rocket's Potato Pockets, and Baby Talk Tacos.
ISBN 0-8118-4419-6
1. Cookery–Juvenile literature. [1. Cookery.] I. Nickelodeon (Firm)
TX652.5.S69 2004
641.5'123–dc22
2003021244

Distributed in Canada by Raincoast Books
9050 Shaughnessy Street, Vancouver, British Columbia V6P 6E5

10 9 8 7 6 5 4 3 2 1

Chronicle Books LLC
85 Second Street, San Francisco, California 94105

www.chroniclekids.com
www.nick.com

# contents

# *welcome to* COOKING 101

*So you want to learn how to knit?* **Sorry. Wrong book.** Want to learn how to measure, mix, and mash your way through the kitchen? **Congratulations!** This is the book for you. But before you make a run for the oven, there are a few important things to remember about working in the kitchen.

## ONE—BE SAFE!

The kitchen is like a laboratory—a place where special equipment is used for (hopefully) successful experiments. You might not wear lab goggles in the kitchen, but safety is still the most important thing. That means *always* asking permission before you start cooking and *always* having an adult nearby to help you. It's especially important that an adult do the dangerous work of using the oven, the stovetop, and any sharp utensils like knives. An adult should also lift heavy pots or pans, especially those containing hot foods or liquids. Here are some more safety tips to follow:

→ Use potholders and oven mitts to handle hot pots, pans, and dishes.

→ Don't touch or lean on surfaces that might be hot, such as the stovetop or oven door.

→ Make sure pot handles don't hang over the edge of the stove; turn them in to the center or to the side.

- Uncover hot saucepans by first tilting up the side of the lid that's farthest away from you; that way you won't get burned by the escaping steam.

- Use only microwave-safe equipment in the microwave oven.

- Don't use electrical appliances near water, and make sure your hands are dry when plugging or unplugging them.

- Never place knives in a sink full of water; you may reach in and cut yourself. Leave them on the counter until you're ready to wash them.

# TWO—BE PREPARED!
Read each recipe carefully *before* you start, to make sure you have all the ingredients and equipment you need. There's nothing worse than diving into a recipe and discovering you only have one egg when you need two. (Squidward hates when that happens.) Reading the recipe first also gives you a chance to become familiar with the steps before you begin. If you come across a word or phrase you don't understand, ask an adult to explain it!

# THREE—BE CLEAN!
There are two parts to being clean in the kitchen. The first and most important part is about making sure that the food you serve is safe and healthy. You do this by always washing your hands before you start to work in the kitchen. You must also remember to carefully clean your hands (and the food prep areas, too) immediately before and after handling raw meat, especially poultry such as chicken and eggs. (When raw, these foods contain a germ called *salmonella* that can make you sick.) The second part of being clean in the kitchen is about keeping things neat! Wear an apron to protect your clothes and have dish towels nearby in case of spills and splatters. If you can arrange it, enlist your own Cosmo or Wanda to help you clean up the kitchen when you're finished cooking. (If you don't have a Cosmo or Wanda, make sure you do it yourself.)

# FOUR—BE HEALTHY!

It makes no difference whether you're the hyper, thrill-seeking type like Sandy Cheeks or the lounge-around-seeking-no-thrills-at-all type like Patrick, your body is your instrument. You've got to treat it right! That means being smart about how you choose to prepare the foods you cook. Substituting some recipe ingredients with the "Healthy Options" suggested throughout this cookbook can lower calories, reduce fat, and even increase nutrients in the dishes you're preparing. Your body will thank you!

# FIVE—BE CREATIVE!

Cooking is an activity that falls some-where between carving like Otto and painting like Picasso. It's an art, and as with all arts you've got to practice to get good at it and most of all use your imagination. Express yourself by putting your own twists on the recipes in this book. Maybe Pasta Squidward would taste better if you added your own seasonings. Or perhaps Wild Boy Berry Waffles should be Wild Boy *Banana* Waffles instead! Practice makes perfect, so start to hone those skills, and don't forget: The most important ingredient in any recipe is always FUN!

# GOBBLE
*and*
# GULP

# baby talk tacos

These tacos are easy to make; just be sure there's enough for Tommy, Chuckie, Phil, Lil, Kimi, Dil, Susie, and Angelica (maybe she'll be nice this time—yeah, right!). Keep all ingredients away from Spike.

1. With an adult's help, follow the directions on the packet of taco seasoning to cook the meat and add the seasoning. Warm the taco shells by following the directions on the package.

2. Place the cooked meat and desired fixings in individual bowls and line them up.

3. Take a couple of taco shells down the assembly line, adding your favorite ingredients. Put on your sombrero and have a fiesta!

Serves 6

**INGREDIENTS**
1 packet taco seasoning mix

1 pound ground beef or ground turkey

1 package taco shells (12 shells)

**FIXINGS**
1 cup grated Cheddar cheese

1 cup shredded lettuce

½ cup chopped onion

1 cup chopped tomato

1 jar hot sauce or salsa

1 large sombrero

CRUNCHY

7

# the crimson chin-ken nuggets

How else do you think the Crimson Chin and Cleft, the Boy Wonder, can battle evil and stay so strong?

**INGREDIENTS**

**1 pound boneless, skinless chicken breasts**

**¼ cup vinaigrette dressing**

**2 cups bread crumbs**

**Salt and freshly ground pepper to taste**

**2 tablespoons olive oil**

**Dipping sauces such as barbecue sauce and honey mustard sauce**

**CRISPY**

1. Ask an adult to cut the chicken breasts into 1-inch-wide strips. Rub vinaigrette into each one.

2. Mix the bread crumbs together with the salt and pepper in a shallow bowl and roll each chicken strip in the mixture until it's evenly coated.

   Have an adult help you with the next two steps.

3. Heat the olive oil in a skillet over medium heat. Gently add the chicken strips and let them cook for about a minute, until the bread crumbs turn golden. Then turn them and cook for about 2 minutes on the opposite side.

4. Lower the heat and continue cooking for about 10 minutes more, turning the strips often. When the chicken is cooked through, remove it from the heat and serve with your favorite sauce to all heroes of the universe!

   Serves 4

# chester cheese pizza

When Chester's freaking out (which is often), a slice of this always saves the day.

1. Preheat the oven to 350°F.

2. Prepare the pizza dough by following the directions on the package. Press out the dough onto a baking sheet.

3. Spread a thin layer of sauce across the dough. Spread the mozzarella and Parmesan cheese on top of the sauce.

4. Sprinkle on your favorite toppings. Have an adult place the pizza in the oven and let it bake for 15 minutes. Don't freak, dude. It's worth the wait.

   Serves 4 to 6

**INGREDIENTS**
1 package pizza dough mix

1 jar of your favorite pizza or spaghetti sauce

2 cups grated mozzarella cheese

½ cup grated Parmesan cheese

Toppings such as peppers, mushrooms, and pepperoni

**HEALTHY OPTIONS**
Use low-fat or part-skim mozzarella and your favorite veggies instead of pepperoni!

# fairly odd pancakes

It's breakfast time and you're craving something different. Nothing satisfies a wish for something new like these pan-tastic pancakes!

**INGREDIENTS**
**2 eggs, lightly beaten**

**1 cup buttermilk**

**1 teaspoon vanilla extract**

**2 cups pancake mix**

**Butter and maple syrup**

**FAIRLY ODD OPTIONS**
**1 cup blueberries**

**1 cup chopped strawberries**

**1 cup chopped walnuts**

**1 cup sliced bananas**

**1 cup chocolate chips**

1. Combine the eggs, buttermilk, and vanilla in a mixing bowl.

2. Add the pancake mix slowly, stirring constantly until all the lumps are gone.

3. Choose your Fairly Odd Options and stir them into the batter.

4. With an adult's help, ladle the batter onto a hot, oiled skillet or griddle in fairly odd shapes (three circles for the snowmen of winter, a circle and two long ovals for the Easter Bunny, or maybe just one big circle … like A.J.'s head!).

5. Cook until the batter begins to bubble, then flip and cook the other side until golden brown. Serve with butter and maple syrup for a truly magical combination!

Serves 4 to 6

FLUFFY

# grilled cheese sandwich,
## *as told by* chef ginger

Everyone at Lucky Junior High agrees: this grilled cheese sandwich RULES!!!

**INGREDIENTS**

**2 slices cheese of your choice**

**2 slices bread**

**2 tablespoons butter**

HEALTHY OPTIONS
Use low-fat cheese and whole wheat bread instead of white!

1. Put the cheese slices between the slices of bread to make a sandwich.

2. Butter the outside of the bread and ask an adult to place the sandwich in a skillet over medium heat.

3. Cook until the bread turns golden brown, then flip the sandwich and repeat. Gobble it up then spread the news of how yummily cheesilicious it is!

Serves 1

So there's this new sandwich in town . . .

. . . it's almost as popular as me . . .

. . . grilled cheese is all the rage!

STRINGY

12

# magic mashers

Wanda's wand puts a whole new spell on potatoes.

1. Use a peeler to peel the potatoes and have an adult cut them into quarters. Put them in a pot and cover them (just barely) with cold water. Bring the water to a boil and let it boil for 15 minutes, or until the potatoes can be easily pierced with a fork.

2. Pour the water out (adults only!) and return the pot to a burner on low heat. Add the milk and butter and start mashing!

3. If you don't have Wanda's magic wand to do the mashing, use a potato masher or a fork. Mash away until the potatoes are nice and smooth, then add salt and pepper to taste. Top with any tasty extras you like, and dig in!

Serves 4

**INGREDIENTS**
**4 medium russet or Idaho potatoes**

**⅓ cup milk**

**2 tablespoons butter**

**Salt and pepper to taste**

**Toppings such as sour cream, chopped chives or green onion, and cooked bacon**

**HEALTHY OPTIONS**
Use skim or low-fat milk, and margarine instead of butter. And skip the sour cream and bacon!

# helga's deviled eggs

Helga puts Old Betsy and the Five Avengers to good use when she mixes up a batch of these del*egg*table daytime treats!

**INGREDIENTS**
**4 large eggs**

**3 tablespoons mayonnaise**

**1 teaspoon Dijon mustard**

**Salt and pepper to taste**

**HEALTHY OPTIONS**
Use light mayo and make 'em crunchy by adding sweet pickle and chopped carrots and celery!

1. Place the eggs in a pot and fill the pot with water. Have an adult bring the water to a boil, simmer the eggs for 15 minutes, then carefully pour the water out and let the eggs cool. (Tip: Place the eggs in cold water and they will cool faster.)

2. Peel the shells from the eggs and cut the eggs in half lengthwise. Arrange the halves on a plate.

3. Carefully scoop out the yellow yolks and place them in a bowl. Add the mayo, mustard, salt, and pepper to the yolks. Mash it all together.

4. Use a spoon to plop a dollop of the mashed-up mixture back into the hollow of each egg white, and prepare yourself to taste something that's devilishly delightful!

Serves 2 to 4

SMELLY

CHEESY

# marianne's mac'n'cheez

There aren't any stores in the jungle, so Marianne has to make the Thornberrys' macaroni and cheese from scratch. After tasting it, Eliza knew one thing for certain: mac 'n' cheez tastes good ANYWHERE!

1. Preheat the oven to 350°F and butter a long, shallow baking dish (like a 13-by-9-inch pan).

2. With an adult's help, melt the butter in a big saucepan over low heat. Add the flour slowly while whisking until it's completely combined.

3. Turn up the heat just a bit and add the milk, slowly pouring it in as you whisk. Once it starts to boil, reduce the heat and add the mustard, cayenne, salt, and pepper.

4. Let the mixture simmer, whisking it occasionally, until it begins to thicken. This should take about 2 minutes.

5. Meanwhile, cook the macaroni by following the instructions on the box, undercooking it the teeniest bit.

6. Combine the macaroni, the sauce, the Cheddar cheese, and 1 cup of the Parmesan in a big bowl. Mix it all up and pour it into the baking dish.

7. In a smaller bowl, mix the remaining ⅓ cup Parmesan with the bread crumbs and sprinkle it on top of the macaroni and cheese.

8. Have an adult place the baking dish in the oven and bake for 25 to 30 minutes, or until it is so golden and bubbly that you can't bear to wait another minute.

Serves 4 to 6

**INGREDIENTS**

6 tablespoons unsalted butter

¼ cup plus 2 tablespoons all-purpose flour

4 cups milk

1½ teaspoons dry mustard

¼ teaspoon cayenne, or to taste

Salt and pepper to taste

1 pound elbow macaroni

3 cups coarsely grated extra-sharp Cheddar cheese (about 12 ounces)

1⅓ cups freshly grated Parmesan cheese (about 4 ounces)

1 cup fresh bread crumbs

**HEALTHY OPTIONS**
Use margarine instead of butter and low-fat milk and cheese!

# plankton *in a* blanket

Since plankton is very difficult to fish for (and too hard to find in the grocery store), hot dogs work as a good substitute in this recipe.

**INGREDIENTS**

**1 package plankton bait**

**1 fishing rod**

**Fresh plankton (or 1 package hot dogs)**

**1 package refrigerated croissant dough**

**Garnishes such as mustard, ketchup, or tartar sauce**

**HEALTHY OPTIONS**
**Try reduced fat or fat-free franks!**

FLAKY

1. Go to the nearest ocean, place the plankton bait on the end of your fishing rod, cast your line, and wait. If you sit there for more than an hour and a half and don't catch any plankton, go buy some hot dogs.

2. Preheat the oven to 375°F. Separate the pieces of croissant dough along the perforated lines.

3. Wrap a piece of dough around each plankton/hot dog, and place it on a baking sheet. Ask an adult to place the sheet in the oven and bake for 15 minutes, or until the dough turns golden brown.

4. Garnish with mustard, ketchup, or—if you caught fresh plankton—tartar sauce. Hang a "Gone Fishin'" sign on the front door, and sit back to enjoy your meal.

Serves 4 to 6

# seanut butter *and* jellyfish jelly sandwich

The only time that Jellyfish Jelly tastes better is when it's on a Krabby Patty!

1. If you prefer your SB&JJ toasted, start by toasting the bread.

2. Spread Seanut Butter on one slice and Jellyfish Jelly on the other. Stick the two slices together, and chomp away.

Serves 1

*If you're unable to locate a jar of Seanut Butter, peanut butter will do in a pinch.

**If the pantry is completely out of Jellyfish Jelly, and you just don't have time to take a quick dive down to Bikini Bottom for a fresh batch, your favorite kind of jelly or jam will do (just don't tell SpongeBob).

**INGREDIENTS**
**2 slices of bread**

**1 jar Seanut Butter***

**1 jar Jellyfish Jelly****

**HEALTHY OPTIONS**
**Choose whole wheat bread instead of white!**

# poof-y rice

Cosmo and Wanda got their hands on this recipe. Now, instead of looking like normal rice, this rice is all puffed up! Or is it "poofed"?

**INGREDIENTS**
**1 cup white rice**

**1 teaspoon salt**

**2 cups boiling water or chicken broth**

HEALTHY OPTIONS
Use brown rice
instead of white!

1. Preheat the oven to 400°F.

2. Pour the rice into a shallow baking pan, making sure it evenly coats the bottom.

3. With an adult's help, place the pan in the oven and bake until the rice turns golden brown. (You'll have to stir it occasionally to keep the rice from sticking to the bottom of the pan)

4. Spoon the rice into a casserole dish that has a snug lid. Don't forget: This rice really e-x-p-a-n-d-s, so make sure the dish is large enough to contain it. Ask an adult to help you choose the right size dish.

5. Add the salt and the boiling water or chicken broth.

6. Cover and bake for 20 minutes. It's so good that—POOF!—it will vanish in minutes!

Serves 4

POOF!

POOF!

PUFFY

# reggie rocket's potato pockets

Reggie's rippin' recipe keeps the gang fueled up for all their adventures.

## INGREDIENTS

**3 whole russet potatoes, cleaned and dried**

**Olive oil**

**5 bacon slices**

**1¼ cups grated sharp Cheddar cheese**

**1¼ cups grated Monterey Jack cheese**

**¼ cup milk**

**1 tablespoon butter**

**¼ teaspoon pepper**

**Salt to taste**

**Toppings such as chopped green onions and sour cream**

**HEALTHY OPTIONS
Skip the bacon and use low-fat cheese, milk, and sour cream!**

1. Preheat the oven to 425°F.

2. Rub the potatoes with olive oil, prick each potato a couple of times with a fork, and place them on a baking sheet. Have an adult put them in the oven to bake for 1 hour, or until tender.

3. Ask an adult to cook the bacon by following the directions on the package. Chop it up and mix it together in a bowl with the Cheddar and Monterey Jack cheese.

4. When the potatoes are cooked, remove them from the oven with an adult's help, and turn the oven off. Allow them to cool, then cut them in half lengthwise.

5. Using a spoon, scoop out most of the potato pulp from the skin, leaving ¼ inch of potato attached. Mix the pulp together with the milk, butter, pepper, and salt in a bowl, then spoon the mixture back into the potato skins.

6. Turn the oven on to 425°F. Sprinkle the cheese and bacon on top of each potato, and put them back in the oven for 25 to 30 minutes. After baking, you can plop a spoonful of sour cream and sprinkle some chopped green onions on top if you like. You might want to put on your helmet before you taste these—they're so delicious you'll be bouncing off the walls!

Serves 3 to 6

# seaworthy cheeseburger

Mr. Krabs just gave SpongeBob this new recipe he wants to try out at The Krusty Krab. Take it for a test run!

1. Season the ground beef or turkey with salt and pepper, and divide it into 4 sections.

2. Shape each section into a patty (a patty is a flattened-out ball—think of a jelly doughnut) and set aside.

3. Ask for an adult's help to melt the butter and oil in a skillet over medium-high heat; once it starts to sizzle, it's time to get cooking! Place the patties in the pan and cook them for 3 to 6 minutes on each side, flipping them over with a spatula.

4. When the burgers are almost done, put a slice of cheese on each and let it melt.

5. If you like your bun toasted, pop it in the toaster while the patty is still cooking.

6. Garnish the burgers with your favorite toppings.

Serves 4

**INGREDIENTS**
**1 pound ground beef or ground turkey**

**Salt and pepper to taste**

**1 tablespoon butter**

**1 tablespoon cooking oil**

**4 slices of cheese**

**4 hamburger buns**

**Toppings such as lettuce, sliced tomatoes, ketchup, pickles, whatever you want!**

**HEALTHY OPTIONS**
Choose ground turkey, use low-fat cheese, and try whole wheat instead of white hamburger buns!

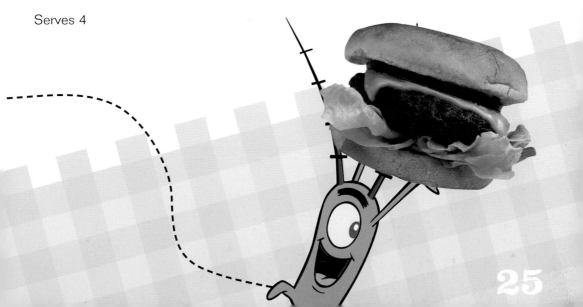

# wild boy berry waffles

You can find two things in the rain forest of Borneo: wild boys named Donnie and lots of berries!

**INGREDIENTS**
**1 package frozen waffles (you'll need 2 per person)**

**2 cups of your favorite berries**

**Maple or berry syrup**

**Loincloth-like pajamas (If none are available, feel free to leap around and squeal like Donnie anyway)**

1. Toast the waffles by following the instructions on the box.

2. Put half of the waffles on individual plates. Cover each waffle with heaps of berries.

3. Put a second waffle on top of the berries and top with syrup.

4. If you're feeling especially wild, pick up your waffles and eat them like a sandwich (although you may have to run that one by the head zookeeper).

Serves 4 to 6

# tito's hula cocktail

Tito is surfin' up a new appetizer for The Shore Shack menu. Like many of his concoctions, this one has some Hawaiian island flavor in the mix.

1. Rinse the cooked shrimp under cold water and place on a paper towel to dry.

2. Place the shrimpy cocktail bowls in a row and pour ¼ cup of the cocktail sauce into each. Place 1 pineapple chunk in the center of each bowl, for extra island flavor.

3. Hook the shrimp all the way around the lips of the bowls, so they look like they're about to dive into the cocktail sauce.

4. Don your diving mask and serve. Dip the shrimp in the cocktail sauce and allow each one a short swim before gobbling. Throw the shrimp tails out to the surf.

Serves 4

**INGREDIENTS**

**1 pound fresh or thawed frozen cooked and peeled shrimp**

**4 shrimpy cocktail bowls**

**1 jar (8 ounces) cocktail sauce**

**4 pineapple chunks**

**1 diving mask**

FISHY

# x-treme scrambled eggs

Grab a whisk and attack some gnarly eggs to create the ultimate br-egg-fast!

**INGREDIENTS**
**4 eggs**

**2 tablespoons milk***

**¼ teaspoon salt**

**⅛ teaspoon pepper**

**2 tablespoons butter**

**Mix-ins such as chopped veggies and grated cheese**

HEALTHY OPTIONS
Use low-fat or skim milk and margarine instead of butter!

**FLUFFY**

1.  Whisk the eggs, milk, salt, and pepper together in a medium bowl.

2.  Ask an adult to help you heat the butter in a skillet over low heat. Once the butter has completely melted, pour in the egg mixture and stir often to cook.

3.  For something different, try adding your favorite chopped vegetable or grated cheese to the eggs. If it's a veggie you're craving, add it to the egg mixture before you pour it in the pan. If it's cheese that pleases you, add it while cooking the eggs, after they have begun to thicken.

4.  Cook the eggs to be as runny or firm as you like them. If Sam were standing by, he'd caution you not to overcook them. That's like missing the ultimate wave!

Serves 2 to 3

*If you want your eggs as light and fluffy as fresh snow, try using 2 tablespoons of water instead of milk.

# pasta squidward

This is Squidward's favorite meal, which he tends to eat alone in his house.

## INGREDIENTS

**1 pound pasta (your favorite kind, of course)**

**2 tablespoons olive oil**

**1 pound ground beef**

**1 jar spaghetti sauce**

**Grated Parmesan cheese**

**1 octopus named Squidward to tell you how much better he makes this dish**

**HEALTHY OPTIONS
Use ground turkey instead of beef!**

1. With the help of an adult, cook the pasta by following the instructions on the bag.

2. Have your grown-up assistant heat the olive oil in a large saucepan over medium heat.

3. Add the ground beef and, using a large wooden spoon, cook and stir it until it all turns brown.

4. Pour the jar of spaghetti sauce over the browned beef and continue to cook until the sauce begins to bubble. (Spaghetti sauce stains are even worse than Jellyfish Jelly stains, so be sure to wear an apron!)

5. Dish out individual plates of pasta and spoon the sauce on top. Garnish with Parmesan cheese and serve while it's hot!

Serves 4 to 6

S A U C Y

# CRUNCH and MUNCH

# drizzled *and* drenched fries

Jimmy likes them drizzled and Sheen likes them drenched.
Carl likes them any way he can get them.

1. Preheat the oven to 325°F.

2. Peel the potatoes, then with an adult's help, cut them
   into long slices that are about $1/2$-inch thick.

3. Arrange the potatoes on a baking sheet in a single layer.
   Pour the olive oil over them and season with salt. Turn so
   that each piece is coated.

5. Cook for 30 minutes at 325°F, then increase the temperature to 400°F and cook for another 30 minutes. Have an
   adult help you turn the fries periodically to make sure
   they brown evenly.

6. While they're still hot, salt the fries and then drizzle them
   with vinegar, according to the demands of your taste
   buds. Pour the ketchup in a bowl, and dip away!

Serves 2 to 4

**INGREDIENTS**
**4 Idaho potatoes**

**½ cup olive oil**

**Salt to taste**

**Malt or balsamic
vinegar**

**Ketchup**

31

# kelp kettle corn balls

Yeeeeehaw! Kelp Kettle Corn Balls are Sandy's specialty. Come 'n' try your hand at these to see just how tasty popcorn can be.

**INGREDIENTS**

⅔ **cup sugar**

½ **teaspoon salt**

⅓ **cup light corn syrup**

**Liquid kelp (a.k.a. green food coloring)**

**8 cups freshly popped popcorn**

1. Ask an adult to help you combine the sugar, salt, and corn syrup in a large pot over medium heat, stirring constantly until the sugar dissolves. (Ask an adult to help you!) Add a few drops of the liquid kelp (or food coloring) and stir until the color of the mixture is even.

2. Reduce the heat and pour the popcorn into the pot. Continue to heat and stir the mixture for 3 or 4 minutes, making sure that all of the popcorn is coated.

3. Remove the pot from the heat and let the mixture cool until you can handle it easily without burning your fingers.

4. Shape it into balls about the size of baseballs.

5. Place the balls on a baking sheet until they've cooled completely. If you manage to resist eating all the balls immediately, store the leftovers by wrapping them in plastic wrap.

Serves 8 to 10

# retroville ranch dip

Jimmy's got an idea for an awesome new invention. It's something that makes vegetables actually taste ... GOOD!

**INGREDIENTS**

**2 cups sour cream**

**1 packet dry ranch dressing mix**

**¾ cup diced tomato**

**¼ cup chopped onion**

**¼ cup chopped olives**

**1 cup grated Cheddar cheese**

**HEALTHY OPTIONS**
Use low-fat sour cream!

1. Mix together the sour cream and the packet of ranch dressing mix in a medium bowl.

2. If sliced and diced extras like tomatoes, onions, olives, and cheese sound tasty, blast 'em in!

3. Chill the dip in the refrigerator for 20 to 30 minutes, and while you're waiting, prepare a plate of Vicky's Not-So-Icky Veggie Sticks (see the next page).

4. Once everything's ready, 3, 2, 1 ... dip away!

Serves 6 to 8

# vicky's *not-so-icky* veggie sticks

Prepare yourself for a big surprise: Vicky can actually do something nice! Because the way she makes vegetables taste, it's almost magic! (Hmmm … maybe Cosmo and Wanda had a hand in this.)

1. Rinse the vegetables.

2. Snap the ends off the green beans and slice the other vegetables lengthwise in strips. Arrange them on a platter.

3. Whip up a batch of Retroville Ranch Dip (see the previous page), and prepare to actually like something that Vicky makes. Who woulda thought?!

Serves 6 to 8

**INGREDIENTS**
**1 bunch carrots, peeled (or 1 bag of baby carrots)**

**1 bunch celery**

**1 cup green beans**

**2 bell peppers**

SNAPPY

# patrick's snack-tricks

Patrick doesn't move too fast, but when it comes to snack cravings, he can snap up a snack quicker than Mr. Krabs rushing toward a dropped penny.

**INGREDIENTS**
**2 flour tortillas**

**2 tablespoons peanut butter**

**2 sliced bananas, 2 sliced apples, or 1 cup raisins**

**2 teaspoons honey**

1. Lay the tortillas flat on a cutting board, and spread a tablespoon of peanut butter on each one.

2. Place the slices of fruit or raisins (or both!) on top, and drizzle each with a teaspoon of honey.

3. Roll up the tortillas and chow down!

4. If you're sharing with your best pal, as Patrick does with SpongeBob, slice the tortillas into 6 sections and enjoy them together.

Serves 2

**SNACKY**

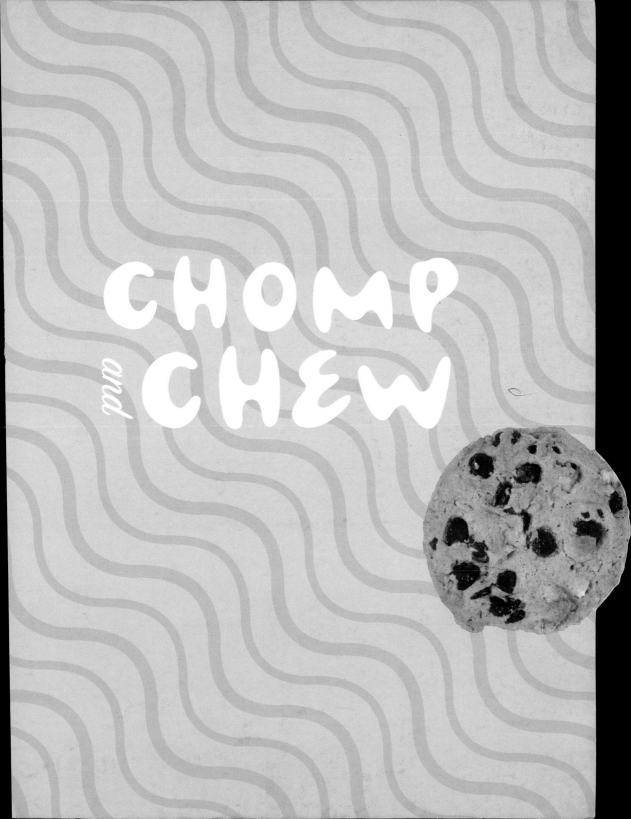

# CHOMP and CHEW

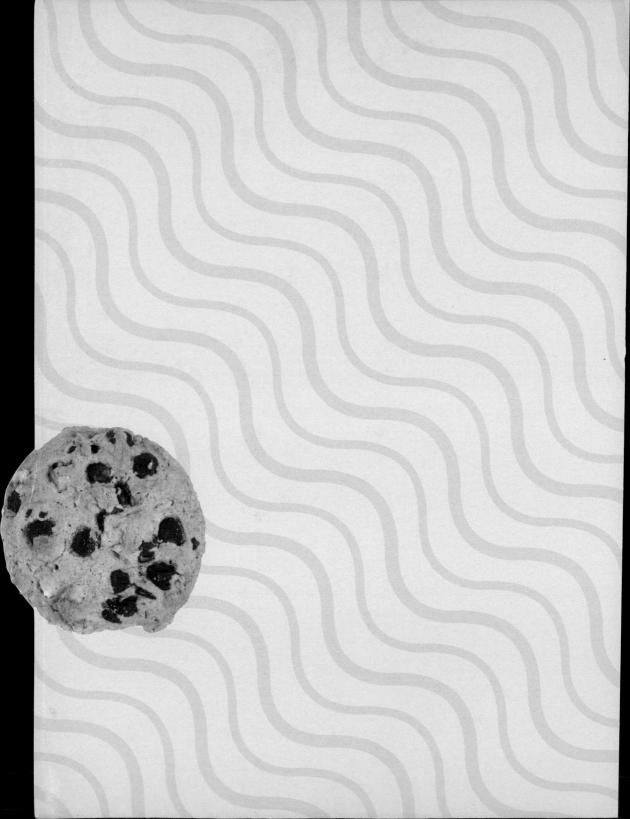

# a.j.'s gelatin delight

A.J. knows a lot. For one, he knows this is the best recipe of all. You'll have to make it yourself to believe him!

1. Pour the gelatin into a medium bowl and carefully add the boiling water (adults only!), stirring constantly until the gelatin dissolves completely.

2. Stir in the cold water, then add the fruit. Ladle the fruity gelatin into individual bowls, or fancy glasses, like A.J.'s.

3. Place them in the refrigerator and chill for 1 to 2 hours. When they're calm and cool like A.J., they're ready to be devoured. Ooze a mountain of whipped cream on top, garnish with a piece of fruit, and enjoy!

Serves 4 to 6

**INGREDIENTS**
**1 box (6 ounces) flavored gelatin**

**2 cups boiling water**

**2 cups cold water**

**2 cups chopped fruit, your favorite**

**Whipped cream**

WIGGLY

# bikini bottom butterscotch brownies

SpongeBob made these for Patrick's birthday once. Patrick ate them all and then offered SpongeBob his empty pan. They are that good! (Of course, Patrick will eat anything, but still, they're quite delicious.)

**INGREDIENTS**
**1 package (12 ounces) butterscotch chips**

**1 box brownie mix, mixed according to the instructions on the box, but not baked**

**1 container (16 ounces) chocolate frosting**

1. Stir half the butterscotch chips into the prepared brownie batter.

2. Pour the batter into a baking pan, and with an adult's help, bake according to the instructions on the box.

3. When the brownies are done, let them cool, then spread a layer of chocolate frosting on top. Decorate the frosting with the remaining butterscotch chips. Some possible decorations are a portrait of Gary, SpongeBob's pineapple, or the word "YUM."

Serves 8 to 10

39

# cindy's peppermint fudge

Cindy loves going to Retroville's Candy Bar with her friends. But since the Candy Bar doesn't make mint fudge, Cindy had to invent an out-of-this-world recipe all by herself (with some help from Libby, of course). Check it out!

1. Ask an adult to help you mix together the sugar, evaporated milk, butter, and salt in a saucepan over medium heat.

2. Bring the mixture to a boil, and stir constantly for 5 minutes.

3. Remove from the heat and stir in the marshmallows, chocolate chips, vanilla extract, and peppermint extract. Continue stirring until the marshmallows are completely melted.

4. Pour the mixture into a foil-lined 8-inch-square baking pan and allow it to cool for several minutes.

5. Sprinkle the crushed peppermint onto the top and press the candy pieces into the fudge lightly so the red and white still shows. Refrigerate for 2 hours.

6. Cut it into squares, and don't offer any to Jimmy.

   Serves 8 to 12

**INGREDIENTS**

1⅔ cups sugar

⅔ cup evaporated milk

2 tablespoons unsalted butter

¼ teaspoon salt

2 cups miniature marshmallows

1½ cups chocolate chips

½ teaspoon vanilla extract

¼ teaspoon peppermint extract

¼ cup crushed peppermint candy

# chocolate chip attack cookies

Beware of falling chocolate chips! These cookies have an avalanche of yummy chocolate flavor.

**INGREDIENTS**

2¼ cups all-purpose flour

1 teaspoon baking soda

1 teaspoon salt

1 cup unsalted butter, at room temperature

¾ cup white (granulated) sugar

¾ cup packed brown sugar

1 teaspoon vanilla extract

2 large eggs

1 package (12 ounces) chocolate chips

1. Preheat your Commvee oven to 375°F.

2. Mix the flour, baking soda, and salt together in a small bowl.

3. Mix the butter, white sugar, brown sugar, and vanilla together in a larger bowl. The mixture should be soft and creamy. (If you have one, use an electric mixer for this. But let an adult help you so it doesn't go flying!)

4. Add the eggs to the butter mixture, then slowly stir in the flour mixture.

5. Now it's time for the showstopper: mix in the chocolate chips.

6. Once everything is completely combined, scoop tablespoon-sized hunks of dough onto a baking sheet and bake for 8 to 10 minutes. Watch out for Donnie! He's been known to eat entire batches at a time.

Serves 8 to 12

**YUMMY**

# gary's globs

*Meow!* Most snails don't go for this chocolaty treat, but it happens to be Gary's all-time favorite.

1. Line a baking sheet with waxed paper.

2. Get an adult's help to melt the chocolate chips in a large saucepan over medium-low heat. Be careful not to burn it! Mix in the crispy Chinese noodles. Add the marshmallows now if you're making Gary's Globbier Globs.

3. Glob spoonfuls of the mixture onto the waxed paper and place the baking sheet in the refrigerator for 1 hour. It will take all of your powers to resist eating the whole batch in one sitting!

Serves 8 to 12

**INGREDIENTS**
**1 cup chocolate chips**

**2 cups crispy Chinese noodles**

**1 cup marshmallows (if you'd prefer to make Gary's Globbier Globs)**

# green slime birthday cake

The best birthday present of all: your very own batch of green slime!

**INGREDIENTS**
**1 box yellow cake mix, plus ingredients listed on back of box**

**1 large box (5.9 ounces) instant vanilla pudding mix, plus ingredients listed on back of box**

**Green food coloring**

**1 cup (½ pint) well-chilled heavy cream**

**1 tablespoon sugar**

**1 teaspoon vanilla extract**

1.  With an adult's help, bake the cake in 2 layers according to the directions on the box. You'll need 2 round 8- or 9-inch cake pans for this.

2.  Make the pudding, following the instructions on the pudding box, and add 8 to 12 drops of green food coloring while blending the ingredients. Cover the pudding, and place it in the refrigerator for at least 1 hour.

3.  Mix the cream, sugar, vanilla, and 8 to 12 drops of green food coloring in a medium bowl, using an electric mixer. Whip the mixture until it forms soft peaks.

4.  Place one layer of the cake on a serving plate, with the bottom side up (be careful when transporting the cake, especially if it's still warm). Spread the whipped cream over it in a thick and even layer. Then place the second cake layer on top, with the top side up.

5.  Cover and refrigerate the cake until it's birthday time.

6.  Bring the cake to the table and uncover it. Pour the slime concoction (or pudding) into a plastic bag that can be sealed and unsealed.

7.  Seal the bag, leaving only a 2-inch opening. Tape the edge of the opening to ensure that the slime won't gush out all at once.

8.  Bring the bag of slime to the table and let everyone take turns sliming the cake!

Serves 10 to 12

SLIMY

48

# timmy's mom's apple pie

Timmy's mom doesn't need magic to make her famous apple pie taste delicious (although Timmy does wish she would make it more often).

1. Preheat the oven to 350°F.

2. Line a pie pan with one of the refrigerated piecrusts, following the instructions on the package.

3. With an adult to assist you, peel, core, and slice the apples. Mix together the sugar, salt, cinnamon, nutmeg, and flour in a large, shallow bowl.

4. Roll the apple slices in the sugar mixture until they are evenly coated, then put them in the piecrust and cover them with the remaining crust.

5. Pinch the two crusts together around the edges of the pie pan, and make a few holes in the top crust with a fork.

6. Let an adult place the pie in the oven and bake for 35 to 40 minutes. Then take a peek at the pie. The crust should be golden brown and the apples should be tender.

7. Use a dull knife to check the apples—they should slice easily. If the apples are still firm but the crust is already brown, place foil over the crust and bake for 5 more minutes, then check again.

8. When the pie is ready to come out of the oven, grab some plates and forks and go to town. To make apple pie á la mode, just plop a scoop of vanilla ice cream on top of each slice.

Serves 6 to 8

**INGREDIENTS**
**2 refrigerated piecrusts (1 box usually contains 2 crusts)**

**6 to 8 large, firm apples**

**1 cup sugar**

**¼ teaspoon salt**

**1 teaspoon ground cinnamon**

**⅛ teaspoon ground nutmeg**

**2 tablespoons all-purpose flour**

F
R
U
I
T
Y

# pineapple pudding under *the* sea

SpongeBob made this for his famous house party (too bad he got locked out of his house and missed the party).

## INGREDIENTS

**1 large box (5.9 ounces) instant chocolate or vanilla pudding mix, plus ingredients listed on back of box**

**1 whole pineapple**

**1 small drink umbrella**

**Hawaiian music**

**SLUDGY**

1. With an adult's help, prepare the pudding mix by following the directions on box.

2. Cut the pineapple in half lengthwise and remove the core. Hollow out the pineapple, and cut the pulp (the fruit part) into small bites. This step is for adults only!

3. Pour the pudding into the hollowed-out pineapple and refrigerate until the pudding sets (a couple of hours or overnight).

4. Once the pudding has set, stir in some pineapple bites, place the small umbrella on top of the pineapple, put on some Hawaiian music, and enjoy!

Serves 4 to 6

# wanda's wacky sundaes

Could Timmy dream up anything more magical than this gooey treat?

**INGREDIENTS**
**1 quart of your favorite ice cream**

**1 cup caramel syrup**

**1 cup chocolate syrup**

**2 bananas, sliced**

**5 strawberries, sliced**

**10 gummy bears**

**1 cup miniature marshmallows**

**3 party hats**

**3 large napkins**

HEALTHY OPTIONS
Use low-fat ice cream!

1. Scoop the ice cream into 3 bowls.

2. Drizzle with caramel and chocolate syrup. Top with banana and strawberry slices. Sprinkle with gummy bears and marshmallows. Put on the party hats. Tuck the napkins into your shirts (thinking about mom here). Dig in!

Serves 3

# GULP *and*
# GUZZLE

# after-ski cocoa

This is Otto, Reggie, Twister, and Sam's favorite treat after carving through some fresh snow on the slopes.

1. Pour the package of cocoa mix into a mug.

2. Bring the water to a boil and put on your ski goggles. Let an adult pour the steamy water over the cocoa. Wipe the steam from your goggles and stir well.

3. Add marshmallows and a peppermint stick, and sip away. After one cup you'll be ready to hit the slopes all over again.

   Serves 1

**INGREDIENTS**
**1 individual packet hot cocoa mix**

**1 cup water**

**1 pair ski goggles**

**A few miniature or regular marshmallows**

**1 peppermint stick**

**HEALTHY OPTIONS**
For a calcium boost, use low-fat or skim milk instead of water!

**STEAMY**

# cosmo's chocolate shake
## *(not snake!)*

Sometimes it's hard to guess why Wanda loves Cosmo so much. With just one taste of his famous chocolate shake, it's magically apparent!

**INGREDIENTS**
**1 cup milk**

**2 tablespoons chocolate syrup**

**2 scoops vanilla ice cream**

**HEALTHY OPTIONS**
**Use low-fat milk and ice cream!**

1. Put the milk, chocolate syrup, and ice cream in a blend With an adult's help, mix on medium to high speed unti liquefied.

2. Pour immediately into a glass. If you like your shakes thick, mix for less time in the blender and devour with spoon instead. Make a wish that you can have second

Serves 1

# exotic fruit smoothie

Nothing quenches Nigel's thirst after a long day in the jungle like an Exotic Fruit Smoothie.

1. With your grown-up partner standing by, put the fruit, milk, yogurt, and ice cubes in a blender, place the cover on the blender, and pull on your E.F.S. safety glasses. Now hit purée! It should take only a minute or so for everything to go wild and get smooth.

2. Pour into a canteen, or a tall glass will do. Keep the safety glasses on, grab a mosquito net, and go out in the wild (or your backyard) to slurp away.

Serves 1

**INGREDIENTS**
2 cups of your favorite fruit (sliced, diced, or chopped)

¼ cup milk

½ cup vanilla yogurt

4 ice cubes (5 if your ice maker makes cubes smaller than your thumb)

1 pair Exotic Fruit Smoothie (E.F.S.) safety glasses (a pair of sunglasses will do in a pinch)

HEALTHY OPTIONS
Use low-fat milk and yogurt!

FOAMY

# serengeti soda

Darwin has sophisticated tastes, and he loves it when Eliza makes this special drink just for him.

**INGREDIENTS**
**3 limes**

**3 tablespoons sugar**

**1 cup club soda or seltzer water**

**1 scoop rainbow or lime sherbet or sorbet**

**Maraschino cherries**

**1 exotic stuffed animal**

**1 pair of binoculars**

1.  Cut each lime in half (let an adult handle the sharp knives!) and squeeze the juice into a measuring cup until you have ¾ cup juice.

2.  Combine the juice and sugar in a small pitcher, stirring with a wooden spoon until the sugar dissolves.

3.  Add the club soda or seltzer water and stir some more. If it's not sweet enough, add more sugar.

4.  Place the sherbet in a tall glass. Pour the juice mixture over the sherbet and garnish with cherries.

5.  Place an exotic stuffed animal nearby and put the binoculars around your neck. Sip your soda and beware of wild beasts!

Serves 1

FIZZY